THE ANIMALS OF FARTHING WOOD

The Adventures of Toad

Colin Dann
Adapted by Clare Dannatt
Licensed by WDR

RED FOX

The evening sun shone brightly on Farthing Wood. It shone on fallen trees and trampled grass. It shone on Toad, struggling to climb over mounds of earth and stones.

'Can't wait to get to the old pond,' he panted.

He had had a long journey home. He was too hot and tired to notice the digging machine behind him, until a giant scoop grabbed the earth underneath him. Toad felt himself rising and falling, and earth tumbling about him.

'Help! I'm being buried! Goodbye, pond!'

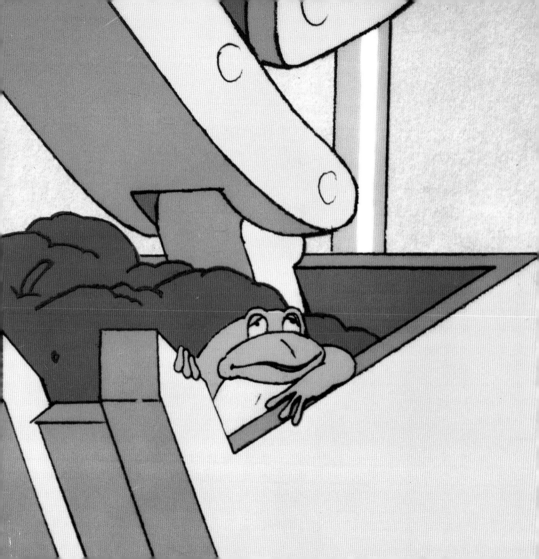

Toad lay still for a while.

'Well, I'm alive,' he thought. It was hard work wriggling out of the heavy earth piled on top of him. Finally Toad broke free, and looked about him cautiously. The sun had set, and the machines were quiet.

'Now for the pond!' croaked Toad.

'I can't hear any birds, or Badger, or the rabbits,' worried Toad as he hopped along. Suddenly he felt himself sinking down into soft ground.

'Oh no, not again,' he groaned. 'Here we go!'

The ground gave way, and Toad landed with a bump. He had fallen into Badger's sett! All the animals of Farthing Wood were round him.

'Where've you been?' asked Weasel.

'A child caught me in a jam jar,' explained Toad, 'and I escaped miles away – but I made it back to the pond!'

'The pond has gone,' said Badger. 'The humans filled it in. They're destroying the wood. And we've got nowhere to go.'

There was silence and then Toad gave a little hop. 'I know a safe place, called White Deer Park. I passed through it on my journey. I'll guide you there.'

'Hooray!' they all cried. 'Let's go tonight.'

As the church bell rang out midnight, Toad hopped to the Great Beech. All the animals were gathered there.

'How do we know you're not inventing this White Deer Park?' Adder asked Toad.

'You might have dreamed it,' put in Weasel.

Toad gulped. Being a guide was hard work.

'I'm sure we can trust Toad,' said Fox, the animals' leader.

Toad felt happy again. 'Everybody ready?' he called. And with one giant leap he led the way.

At dawn the travelling animals came to a big road. They scampered, hopped and crawled across as fast as they could.

But Toad was exhausted. The road hurt his feet. Then, drowning the shouts of encouragement from his friends, he could hear the roar of a lorry!

He couldn't hop any faster. Now he could see the shadow of the lorry, and feel its hot breath. He gave one short hop, and closed his eyes.

The lorry stopped. Toad breathed again – he wasn't going to be run over. But then the driver stepped down to the road. Toad flopped, pretending to be dead. He winced when a boot prodded him. Would he be squashed after all?

Toad heard a hooting and a flapping, and shouting.

Owl had attacked the human!

Then Toad saw Fox next to him.

'Quick,' whispered Fox in Toad's ear, 'hold on to my tail.' And so Toad was whisked to safety.

'Thanks Fox, thanks Owl,' he gasped. 'Thanks for saving my life.'

But even after a rest, Toad couldn't keep up with the other animals.

'The guide shouldn't be at the back,' he muttered. 'Awfully hot, too, eh Adder?'

'Yessss,' hissed Adder, and then stopped. 'There's a fire ahead!'

Toad's eyes bulged as flames flickered towards him. Adder slithered away quickly.

'I can't move,' gasped Toad.

He heard a call. 'I'm here,' he croaked – but no voice came out. A tear rolled down his cheek. Then Fox was running towards him through the burning bushes.

Fox picked Toad up gently in his mouth and ran with him through the flames. Gradually it grew cooler, and Toad felt strong enough to travel on Fox's back. He clung on tight as they galloped through the marsh. At last Toad could see some familiar shapes dimly through the smoke. All the animals were waiting for them.

'Here come Toad and Fox!' cried Badger. 'Our guide and our leader are safe.'

And so all the animals were able to continue on their journey.

Toad was happy when they reached a river. But not all the animals liked getting wet and they worried about crossing the river.

'We'll be safe,' boasted Toad as he jumped in. 'I'll show you.'

Cautiously the other animals followed him. But the rabbits panicked. Fox did his best to save them – only to be swept away in the current by a mass of branches.

'We'll have to go on without Fox,' decided Badger after a long wait for him.

'Follow me,' said Toad, hopping sadly away from the river he had thought would be such fun.

The animals travelled on many miles. Fox had managed to escape from the river further down and had found the others again, so everyone was happy.

But Toad needed water desperately. When they reached a quarry, he plunged straight in to the pond.

'Hurry up, you lot,' he called, as he swam about. 'It's lovely!'

But all of a sudden, Toad started to struggle.

'Help!' he called. 'Something's got me!'

And splashing and shrieking, Toad disappeared under the water.

A big fish's jaws had clamped around Toad's head. 'I've really had it this time!' he thought.

Then, as he kicked out with his legs, he felt himself shooting back up through the water and into the air above.

He was on dry land, and someone was dragging him out of the fish's mouth. Toad blinked and gasped for air.

'You'll be all right,' said a giant bird towering above him – it was Whistler, a heron. 'Saw you in trouble – thought I'd help out.'

Once again, Toad had been rescued. And so Whistler joined the animals on their journey to White Deer Park.

'There's a road ahead,' called Kestrel one morning. 'A really big one this time – a motorway!'

The animals gazed hopelessly at the traffic. 'We larger animals can dash across,' said Fox. 'But the small ones will never make it.'

'No problem,' said Whistler. 'I'll carry them in my beak.'

Toad shivered – but remembered how Whistler had helped him before. 'I'll go first,' he volunteered. Whistler scooped him up – and Toad was flying over the traffic. It was almost as good as swimming!

The animals were very near White Deer Park now.

'We'll be there in two hops,' said Toad, leading the way through a gap in a hedge. 'We are – we're here!'

Toad looked about him – and met the gaze of a huge white stag.

'Well done, Toad,' boomed the stag. 'Welcome, animals of Farthing Wood.'

'Three cheers for our guide, Toad,' the animals yelled.

Toad looked shy. 'Thanks, friends. Now we can all live peacefully in our own way.' And Toad smiled happily at the thought of the beautiful pond in White Deer Park.

A RED FOX BOOK
Published by Random House Children's Books
20 Vauxhall Bridge Road, London SW1V 2SA

A division of Random House UK Ltd
London   Melbourne   Sydney   Auckland   Johannesburg
and agencies throughout the world

First published by Red Fox 1992

Based on the animation series produced by Telimagination/La Fabrique
for the European Broadcasting Union
from the series of books about
The Animals of Farthing Wood by Colin Dann

Printed and bound in Belgium by Proost International Book Production

ISBN 0 09 920481 9